A suitcase of seaweed

and other poems

Also by Janet S. Wong
Good Luck Gold and Other Poems

A suitcase of seaweed

and other poems

Janet S. Wong
Decorations by the author

Margaret K. McElderry Books

To Andrew

AUTHOR'S NOTE: Now and then you may wonder why I put a poem in one part of this book rather than another. Sometimes the reason is as small as one word, or my memory of a certain salty smell.

Margaret K. McElderry Books
An imprint of Simon & Schuster Children's Publishing Division
1230 Avenue of the Americas
New York, NY 10020

Book design by Becky Terhune
The text of this book was set in Bembo
Printed in the United States of America

First Edition
10 9 8 7 6 5 4 3 2 1

Library of Congress Cataloging-in-Publication Data
Wong, Janet S.
A suitcase of seaweed and other poems / Janet S. Wong.—1st ed.
p.   cm.
Summary: A collection of poems that reflect the experiences of Asian Americans, particularly their family relationships.
ISBN 0-689-80788-0
1. Asian American families—Juvenile poetry. 2. Asian American children—Juvenile poetry. 3. Family—United States—Juvenile poetry. 4. Asian Americans—Juvenile poetry. 5. Children's poetry, American. [1. Asian Americans—Poetry. 2. Family life—Poetry. 3. American poetry.] I. Title.
PS3573.0578S85   1996   811'.54—dc20   95-38282   CIP   AC

This book was made possible in part by a grant from the Society of Children's Book Writers and Illustrators.

Contents

Part 1: Korean Poems

Part 2: Chinese Poems

Part 3: American Poems

PART I

Korean Poems

Garlic Boat   JW

My mother is Korean. She came to this country in 1960, married to my father, who met her when he was stationed in Korea with the U.S. Army. I still am not sure how they met, exactly. Something about him buying food for the troops, and her selling food from her farm. How could they fall in love, since she could not speak any English and he could not speak Korean? He married her for her nose, he says. It is a pretty nose, short and thin, pointed, straight. I have my father's nose.

Growing up, I never felt very Korean. My Korean aunt and grandparents lived in this country for only a few years, when I was in high school. And I visited Korea only once, when I was four. The month I was there I learned to speak enough Korean to order ice cream at the train station. It was the best ice cream I have eaten in my whole life.

Lately I have been wanting to know more about my mother, and for the first time I find myself craving Korean beef bone soup and *kimchi*, which I used to hate. Now I can eat the hottest *kimchi* without wincing. I eat it whenever I like, not caring about garlic breath, even turning down the gum the waitress offers when you pay the bill. Gum won't work, anyway, once garlic gets in your blood.

Love at First Sight

I like to imagine Mother
when her face was full and smooth
and she wore her hair in a long braid,

and I like to imagine Father
with his crooked smile and his crooked crew cut,
wearing an American uniform,

running after her
in the narrow dirt streets
of her Korean village,

as she rushes away
laughing,
her long braid

wagging like the tail of a dog
that has found
a fresh bone.

Burial

We take turns
digging the hole
in the hard dry ground,
pushing the shovel down
in the dirt
with the soles
of our shoes.
The sweat drips
from my forehead
into my eyes
like tears.
Slowly Haraboji
lowers
the large clay
kimchi jar
into the cool dark pit,
this makeshift cellar
where chili peppers
and garlic and cabbage
will mix and sit in salt,
covered
with snow until
spring, when
the *kimchi* is hot enough
to chase away all
trace of winter's
chill.

Leeches

With his cigarette
Uncle Kishunee
burns them off
my legs
one by one,
smearing
their marks
with mud.

Then he carries me
home, piggyback,
along river rows
of grassy rice,
his bare feet
sucking
the ground
like leeches.

Acupuncture

"Chook! Chook! Chook!"
Mother says each time
she digs her finger
into my skin
to show me where
the doctor stuck
hundreds of needles
in her swollen, still,
fever-filled body,
when she was twelve.

I have a picture
in my mind
of how she looked—*Chook!*
My mother, once
a porcupine.

A Suitcase of Seaweed

Across the ocean
from Korea
my grandmother,
my Halmoni,
has come—
her suitcase
sealed shut
with tape,
packed full
of sheets
of shiny black
seaweed
and stacks
of dried squid.
We break it open,
this old treasure
chest of hers,
holding
our noses
tight
as we release
its ripe
sea smell.

Campfire

Just think—
when Mother was my age,
she could build a fire
with sparks from rocks,
catch a bunch of
grasshoppers and
roast them whole
for a summer
night's snack!

"Get me a good stick,"
she says, "thin but strong,"
and I bring her one
from the woods
behind our tent.
On the way back
I see a brown bag
by her feet—
could it be?

When the fire is spitting ready,
she reaches
in the bag, rustling,
and hands me
one big, fat, luscious
marshmallow.

Beef Bone Soup

It is three-thirty in the afternoon
at the Korean soup shop. Mother
has ordered her favorite soup,

boiled until the cloudy broth turns
the creamy color of old teeth. I pull
a beard of noodles from the bowl

before I remember we must pray,
and there it stays, dripping,
hanging near my chin, while

Mother bows her head. She bends
over the bowl so long and so low
she seems to be steaming

her pores open. My wrist is stiff.
I drop my noodles, hoping she will
get the hint, then I start to play

with the salt and my spoon.
But she remains as she was,
at least one whole minute more,

until I cannot help myself,
and sneak one small early slurp—
so hot it burns my tongue.

Joyce's Beauty Salon

They call my mother
the perm lady, "Pum Ajima."
Dozens of mad Korean women
come in each month, ugly,
furious with their families,
frustrated by their stubborn,
straight, heavy hair.
A few hours with Mother
and they leave
carrying a lighter load,
their carefree curls
bouncing out the door.

Koreatown

Koreatown
is growing

like an amoeba, engulfing
whole streets each week—

> churches
> swap meets
> barbecues
>
> cleaners
> markets
> beauty shops

Koreatown is growing, spreading,

splitting.

Hospitality

My guest
must not have noticed
how I removed my shoes
as we stepped inside my house.

My guest
must have missed
the neat line of freshly shined shoes
near the door.

My guest
apparently did not see
my mother's shock as she watched
his shoes walking toward her,

muck-covered shoes
impossible to ignore
when she offered him
nothing to eat.

Persimmons

Mother tells me, once again,
how *her* mother used to spy
on her, piercing the sliding
rice paper screen with a pin
and peeping through the hole
with her better eye.

That is how Mother, always
so hungry, got caught
stuffing her jacket pockets
full of dried persimmons,
and that is why I get to eat
more than anyone could ever
possibly want.

Rice Cooker

Reaching into the rice bin
with a porcelain bowl
chipped at the rim,
I scoop out
plenty for four
and pour it
in the pot.

Then I wash it,
swishing and rinsing,
careful not to spill
a single grain
down the drain,
swishing and rinsing
until the milky water
runs nearly clear.

I measure the water
with my knuckle,
plug the cooker in,
press the button
and wait, wait, wait—

wait for Mom
to come home.

PART 2

Chinese Poems

Gold Mountain Tea   JW

My father is Chinese. He came to this country when he was twelve. My grandfather came here in the early 1920s. He worked on a farm near Sacramento, California, for eight years, then returned to China for a visit. On that visit he married my grandmother, built a house, and had a baby—my father.

Soon after my father was born, my grandfather, my GongGong, came back to the United States to make money. He worked as a cook in a restaurant in Los Angeles. Just when he had bought a restaurant of his own, he was drafted into the U.S. Army.

After World War II my grandfather brought my grandmother and father to this country. In the 1950s they bought a small restaurant and called it "Wong's Café." I worked there one or two hours a day when I was four, five, and six years old. I would arrive before dark, after I finished sweeping hair from the floor in my mother's beauty shop three doors down. I was not a very good worker and mainly just wiped tables, hiding the tip money in my apron pockets.

I liked to talk to the customers. Albert Bell— my uncle Al—was one of our best customers. One afternoon, before I was born, he found my mother lost on the street. He knew her from the restaurant. She spoke a little English then, but not enough to find the right bus. Al helped her back to the restaurant, where my grandfather scolded her. Uncle Al always left a big tip.

Albert J. Bell

Forty years of friendship
with my grandfather,
and still Uncle Al cannot eat
with chopsticks.

Forty years of friendship
with Uncle Al,
and still my grandfather forgets
to offer him a fork.

Poetry

"What you study in school?" my grandfather asks.

"Poetry," I say, climbing high to pick a large ripe lemon off the top limb.

"Po-tree," he says. "It got fruit?"

When I Grow Up

I want to be an artist, Grandpa—
write and paint, dance and sing.

Be accountant.
Be lawyer.
Make good living,
buy good food.
Back in China,
in the old days,
everybody
so, so poor.
Eat one chicken,
work all year.

Grandpa, things are different
here.

Money Order

We eat salt fish and rice,
night after night after night,
to save some money
to send
to cousins
I never have seen

who used our money last year
to buy a color TV,
so they could watch
rich Americans
eating
steak and potatoes.

Shrimp

Around and around and around it spins
on the lazy Susan,
that last piece of shrimp.
I am too ashamed of my appetite
to look at it again
so instead I force my eyes
to wander, looking at paintings
of fish and crab and   ·
shrimp—
Instead I look at the waiters,
walking from the tanks with nets
of thrashing fish and wriggling
shrimp—
Instead I look around the table,
measuring the hills of peeled shell
piled on my mother's plate,
my father's plate,
my brother's plate—

My brother's plate!

This shrimp is mine!

After a Dinner of Fish

"A surprise for you, from the sea,"
Grandmother whispers, with a wink,
once the dinner dishes are done,
once she has scrubbed the kitchen sink,
once we have made chrysanthemum tea—

now that we are alone.

"Guess," she says, "but do not tell."
She pulls a paper napkin square
from her apron pocket and
puts it in the palm of my hand.
I shut my fingers, like a shell,
around this gift, in its disguise,
knowing what I will find there—

poor girl's pearls, cooked fish eyes.

Tea Ceremony

"This tea costs sixty dollars a pound,"
Grandfather announces, and grunts
as I begin to pour.
This is a signal
for Mother
to look at my free hand,
a glance that lasts
long enough to scold:
Two hands!

Like a puppet
I lift my left hand,
answering her silent command
to hold the lid down,
while my right hand
tips the teapot
toward Grandfather
in a slow, deep bow.

Two hands!
I feel all eyes watching
as I cradle
the old heat-cracked cup
in soft hands of respect,
holding it out to Grandfather
like an offering
to the gods.

GongGong* and Susie

Susie sure is good
watchdog.
Got to be.
I treat her right.
Last night
almost
kill a skunk.

Did I tell you?
Many times
I did eat
skunk
soup.
Take out them
stinky thing,
cook
with garlic, onion.
Skunk, snake, night owl,
I eat them
all.
It was Depression time.
No work, nothing
to do.
We hunt, we fish, we camp.

Hey Susie, Susie,
want to eat
some chow
mein?

*GongGong is one Cantonese word for grandfather.

Sisters

She calls me tofu
because I am so soft,
easily falling apart.

I wish I were tough
and full of fire, like ginger—
like her.

In the Hospital Room

I turn my back
on Grandmother
as the nurse
feeds her
so she does not
see me
peeking
from the corner
of my eye
at her mouth
opening wide,
too wide,
the way a baby
opens his mouth,
not knowing
its size.

Grandmother's Almond Cookies

No need cookbook, measuring cup.
Stand close. Watch me. No mess up.

One hand sugar, one hand lard
(cut in pieces when still hard),

two hands flour, more or less,
one pinch baking powder. Guess.

One hand almond, finely crushed.
Mix it with both hands. No rush.

Put two eggs. Brown is better.
Keep on mixing. Should be wetter.

Sprinkle water in it. Make
cookies round and flat. Now bake

one big sheet at three-seven-five.
When they done, they come alive.

Marathon

I hope the Chinese
wins the race.

I see myself
in her face.

Does she see me
in this crowd?

Does she hear me
cheering loud?

When I am grown
but not too old—

I'll run this race.
And win the gold.

PART 3

American Poems

Half and Half   jw

I am American. I was born here, in Los Angeles, in the old Queen of Angels Hospital, right off the 101 freeway. Four years ago they boarded up the building. I read it might be rented out as a movie studio next year.

Sometimes the first question a stranger will ask me, even before learning my name, is "What are you?" or "Where are you from?" These kinds of people usually stare hard at my face, as if they are testing themselves on how well they can tell the difference between Chinese and Korean and Japanese. Usually I give them what they want to know, quickly, and get it over with. It can be fun, though, to pretend I do not understand.

My mother says when I was six years old I got in a big fight with our neighbors. Carol and Daryl had teased me for being half Chinese and half Korean. They were full-blooded Japanese Americans, and called me a half-breed, a mixed poodle. We *did* have a mixed poodle then, Blackie. My mother says I cried, and she laughs, patting my curly permed hair.

Manners

If you are Chinese
and you eat out of
a porcelain bowl,
you may pick it up
and push the rice
into your mouth
with your chopsticks,
feeling a bit like
a pig, digging in.
But it is okay,
if you are Chinese.

If you are Korean,
though, you must
leave your stainless
steel bowl sitting
on the table, even
if it has gone cold
while you barbecue
beef for your father.

And if you are half
and half, like me,
born in L.A. and hungry
all the time,
you might wonder
if you aren't better off
sticking with
a knife and fork.

Face It

My nose belongs
to Guangdong, China—
short and round, a Jang family nose.

My eyes belong
to Alsace, France—
wide like Grandmother Hemmerling's.

But my mouth, my big-talking mouth, belongs
to me, alone.

Other

We notice each other right away.
We are the only two Asians in the room.
It does not matter that her hair is long.
It does not matter that I am fat.
I look at her like I look in a mirror,
recognizing my self in one quick glance.

Which?

Two dresses hang
side by side
on the sale rack,
the tag of one so worn
it seems the price
was not believed,
but looked at, at least twice,
by many who might buy.

It is real: this
black velvet gown
overgrown with
lush, bright flowers
is cheap, dirt cheap,
even cheaper than
the simple chambray dress
some careless hand
has pressed up against its back,
the white plastic hanger
crushing one velvet flower.

Which one is you?
Wear this plain blue frock
twice a week and feel safe,
no one will talk;
but wear the other,
with its strange power
that makes you think
the boys will swoon,

and a second time
a season
is too soon.

Quitter

Coach calls me a quitter.

He mutters it under his breath
loud enough for me to hear,
but quiet enough
so no one knows
when I prove him wrong.

Our Daily Bread

Nine P.M. we close the store,
wash the counter, mop the floor.

Ten P.M. we finally eat.
Father pulls a milk crate seat

to the table and we pray.
Thank you for this crazy day.

Treat

It's my best friend's treat.
I won our bet.

I'd love the shrimp,
but I think I'll get
the pork instead—
it's half the price.

It's my best friend's treat,
but I'll treat her nice.

Lotto

My brother buys tickets
every Wednesday.
He scrounges change,
rummaging through
coat pockets
and old purses
in the closet,
turning over
couch cushions,
checking the
coin return slots
of copy machines
and pay phones.
We pass a penny,
he picks it up.
And all week long
we wait for luck.

In the Neighborhood

We drove past
our old house
today.
The redwood
fence is warped
and gray.
The tree
I planted
grew so tall
it makes
our house look
plain and small.

When we
lived there,
it was the best.
Now it seems
just like
the rest.

Straight A's

My parents and I
don't talk about grades.
It's understood.
I will get A's.

They never say what
they want me to do.
I wish they would—
I wish I knew.

Beat

When I was small
they spanked me
with a newspaper
rolled tight,
and I would yell
until the neighbors
opened their warped
wooden windows.

Now they have learned
a better way,
and the pain hurts worse
than a whipping
when they shake
their heads, whispering,
"We are so ashamed,"
in a room so quiet
you hear them
swallow.

Quilt

Our family
is a quilt

of odd remnants
patched together

in a strange
pattern,

threads fraying,
fabric wearing thin—

but made to keep
its warmth

even in bitter
cold.